Go, Sled! Go!

James Yang

VIKING

Go, sled! Go!

Sorry,
bunny.

Oh, snowman! No!

Are you okay,
Mr. Snowman?

Oh, moose! No!

GOING DOWN!

What are penguins doing here?

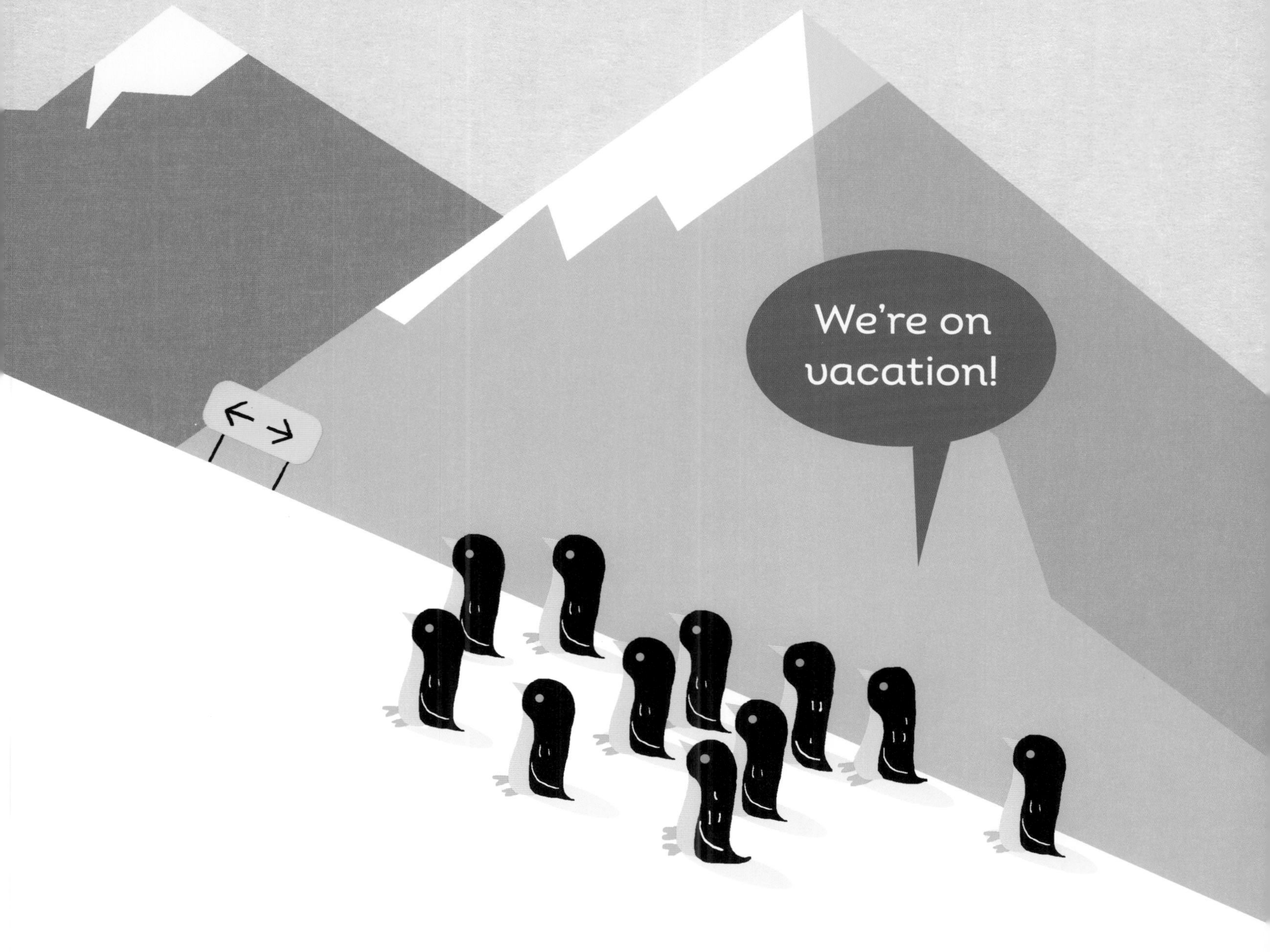

Sorry we took your friend!

Oh,
village!
No!

Jump, sled!

Jump!

SKY VIEW

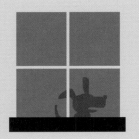

NOOOOOOOOOOOOOOOOOOOOOOO

oooo!

STOP

Stop, sled! STOP!

STOP

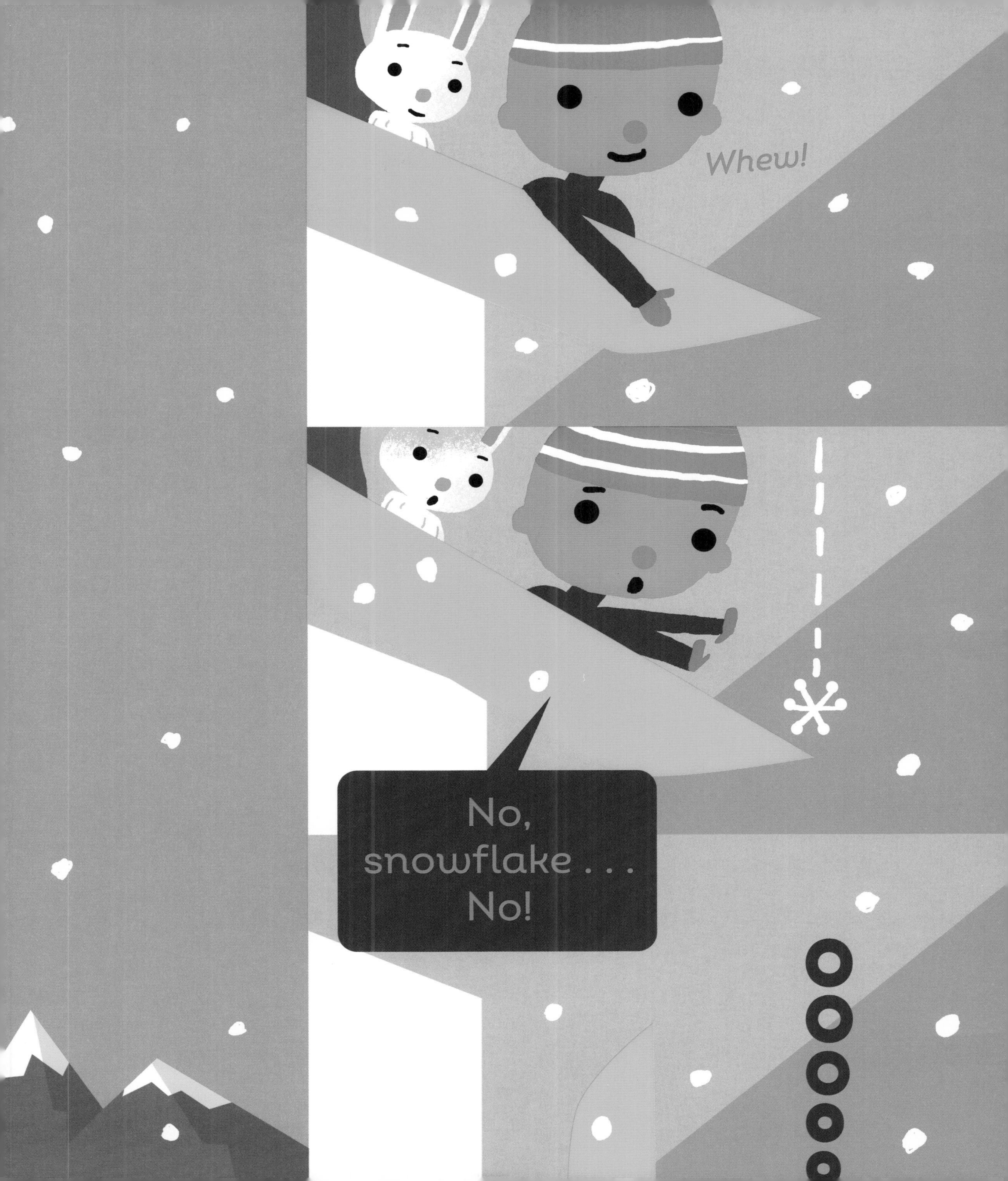
Whew!
No, snowflake . . . No!

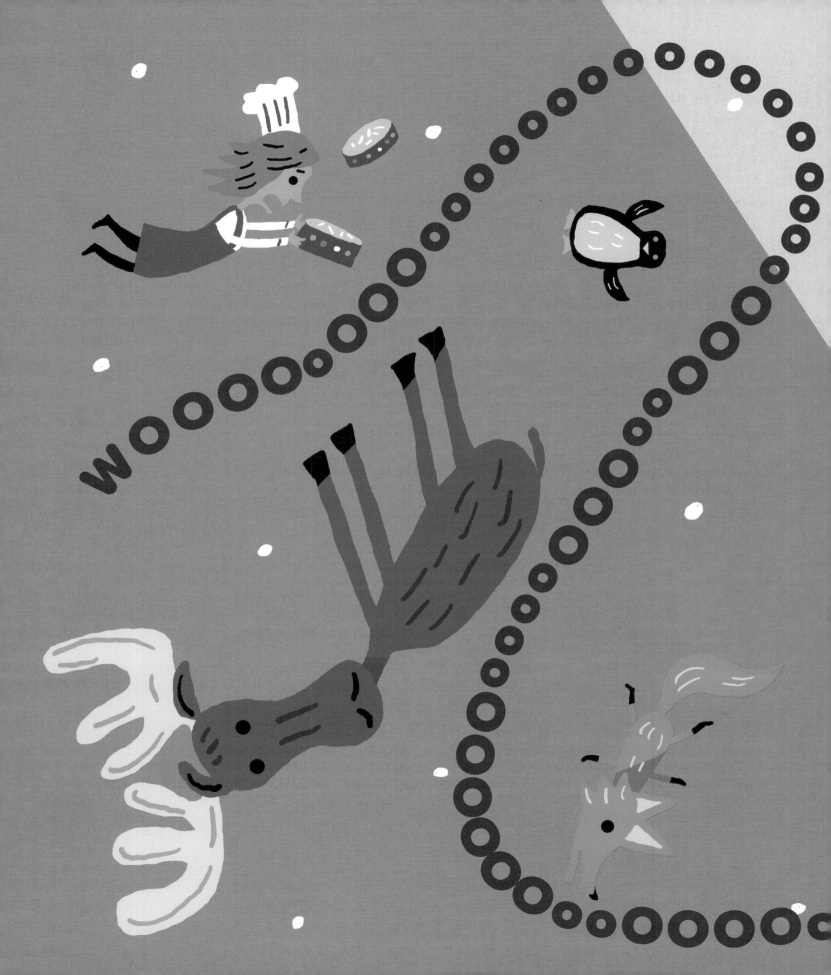

WOOOOOOOO

Dedicated to everyone
I ever sneak-attacked with a snowball.
The memories still warm my heart.

VIKING

An imprint of Penguin Random House LLC, New York

First published in the United States of America by Viking, an imprint of Penguin Random House LLC, 2022

Copyright © 2022 by James Yang

Visit us online at penguinrandomhouse.com.

Library of Congress Cataloging-in-Publication Data is available.

Manufactured in China

ISBN 9780593404799

1   3   5   7   9   10   8   6   4   2

TOPL

Design by Jim Hoover
Text set in Intro Regular and Proxima Soft

The illustrations in this book were created digitally with the aid of hot cocoa and a good pair of warm mittens.